SPECIAL

BY BRIGITTE WENINGER
TRANSLATED BY J. ALISON JAMES

Copyright © 2000 by Nord-Süd Verlag AG, Gossau Zürich, Switzerland
First published in Switzerland under the title WAS KANN DAS SEIN?
English translation copyright © 2000 by North-South Books Inc.

First published in the United States, Great Britain, Canada,
Australia, and New Zealand in 2000 by North-South Books,
an imprint of Nord-Süd Verlag AG, Gossau Zürich, Switzerland.

Distributed in the United States by North-South Books Inc., New York.

Library of Congress Cataloging-in-Publication Data is available.
A CIP catalogue record for this book is available from The British Library.
ISBN 0-7358-1318-3 (trade binding)
1 3 5 7 9 10 8 6 4 2
Printed in Hong Kong

For more information about our books, and the authors and artists
who create them, visit our web site: www.northsouth.com

DELIVERY

ILLUSTRATED BY

ALEXANDER REICHSTEIN

A MICHAEL NEUGEBAUER BOOK, NORTH-SOUTH BOOKS, NEW YORK/LONDON

ne morning the
doorbell rang.

It was the postman bringing
a great big brown box.

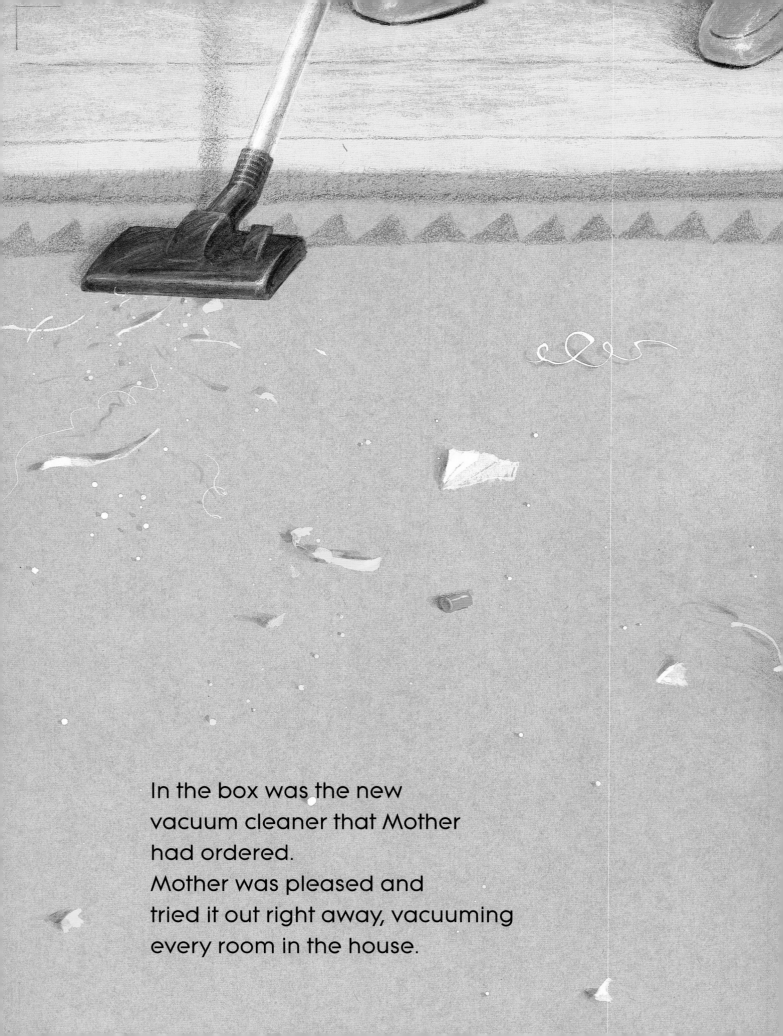

In the box was the new
vacuum cleaner that Mother
had ordered.
Mother was pleased and
tried it out right away, vacuuming
every room in the house.

That afternoon the doorbell
rang again.

Outside stood a great big
painted box.
"What's this?" said Mother.
"Another package?"

She looked to the left.
She looked to the right.
There was no one in sight.

But there on the great
big box were great big letters
that said, quite clearly:
MOTHER

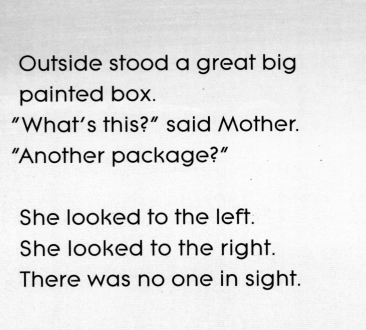

BRUTTO W: 8 KGS
NETTO W: 5 KGS

"Well!" said Mother.
"I am certainly the only
Mother in this house,
so this must be for me!"
She pushed the box
into the hall.

"WHAT COULD IT BE?"

Mother puffed.
"The box is so heavy and
it rumbles like rocks.
Maybe it's full of golden
treasure!
But wait... what's this?"

Mother noticed a
small opening on the side
of the box.
She carefully felt inside.

"WHAT COULD
IT BE?

There is something soft
and furry.
Is it something to cuddle?
Maybe it's a giant
stuffed toy!
But wait... what's this?"

On the other side of the box
was another opening.
Mother put her fingers in.

"WHAT COULD
IT BE?

There is something smooth
and round.
Is it something to play with?
Maybe it's a huge
rubber ball.
But wait... what's this?"

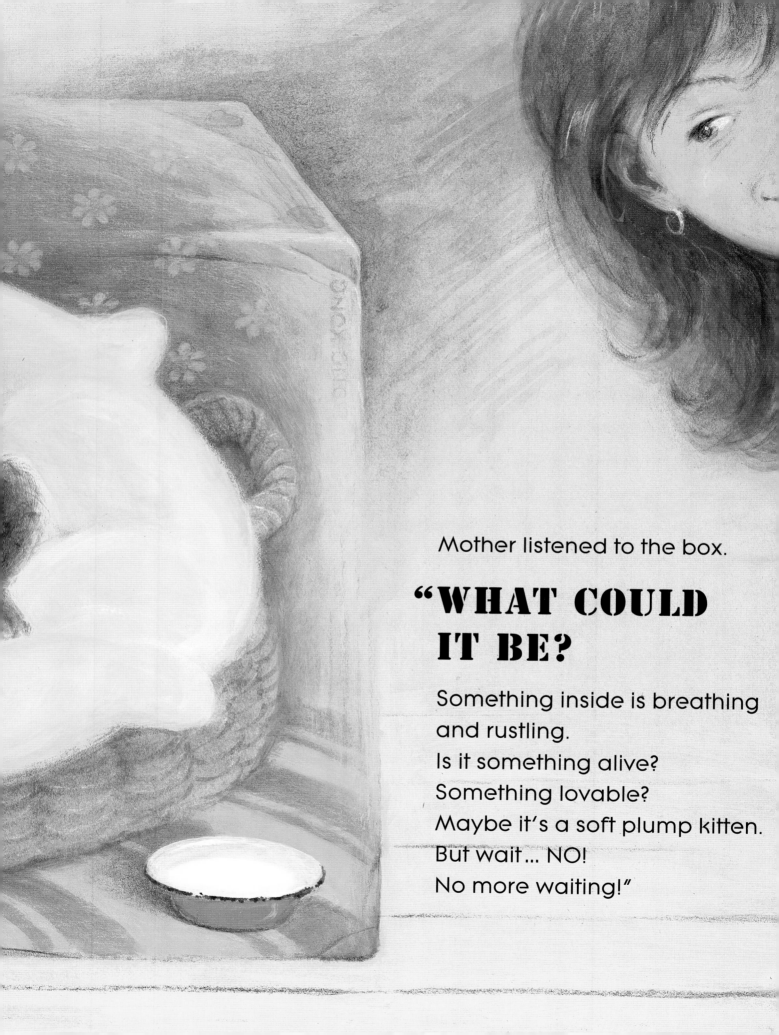

Mother listened to the box.

"WHAT COULD IT BE?

Something inside is breathing
and rustling.
Is it something alive?
Something lovable?
Maybe it's a soft plump kitten.
But wait... NO!
No more waiting!"

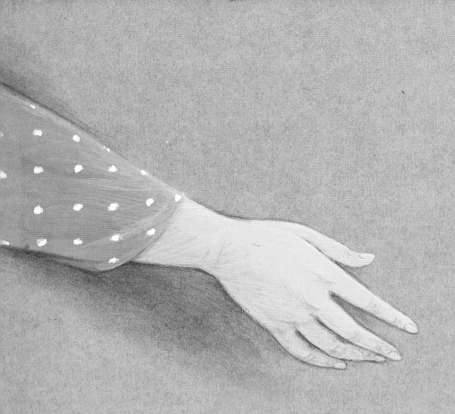

Mother couldn't bear it any longer!
"There must be something very special,
something one of a kind,
something absolutely wonderful
in this box!"

"WHAT COULD IT BE?"